RADSPORTS GUIDES

SNOWBOARDING

TRACY NELSON MAURER

Rourke Publishing LLC
Vero Beach, Florida 32964

www.rourkepublishing.com

Project Assistance:
Jon Strasburg moved to Jackson, Wyoming, after graduating from the University of Wisconsin-Eau Claire. He swabbed the resort toilets at night to pay for his lift tickets during the day. A proven new-school downhill skier and snowboarder, Jon also honed his aggressive mountain-bike riding skills and performed in commercials.

In addition, Joel Rosen at 1080skiboarding.com and Source Skiboarding Apparel in Boston, Mass.; Heidi Jo Viaene, Ski School Director at Spirit Mountain, Duluth, MN; and the staff of Ski Hut in Duluth, MN generously shared their expertise.

The author also extends appreciation to Mike Maurer, Kendall and Lois M. Nelson, and Harlan Maurer.

Photo Credits:
Page 4: © Al Bello/Allsport; Page 8: Elsa Hasch/Allsport; Pages 11, 18, and 39: © Jamie Squire/Allsport; Pages 21 and 27: © Nathan Bilow/Allsport; Pages 24 and 29: © Brian Bahr/Allsport; Page 31: D & P Armentrout; Pages 32 and 35: Al Bello/Allsport; Page 36 Mike Powell/Allsport; Page 43: © Allsport

Editorial Services:
Pamela Schroeder

Notice: This book contains information that is true, complete and accurate to the best of our knowledge. However, the author and Rourke Publishing LLC offer all recommendations and suggestions without any guarantees and disclaim all liability incurred in connection with the use of this information.

Safety first! Activities appearing or described in this publication may be dangerous. Always wear safety gear. Even with complete safety gear, risk of injury still exists.

Library of Congress Cataloging-in-Publication Data

Maurer, Tracy Nelson
    Snowboarding / Tracy Nelson Maurer
     p. cm. — (Radsports guides)
    Includes bibliographical references and index.
    Summary: Surveys the history, equipment, techniques, and safety factors of snowboarding.
    ISBN 1-58952-106-4
    1. Snowboarding—Juvenile literature. [1. Snowboarding.] I. Title: Snowboarding. II. Title

GV857 .S57 M3562001
796.93'9—dc21   2001041650

Printed in the USA

TABLE OF CONTENTS

CHAPTER ONE   GET THE GEEK OUT 5

CHAPTER TWO   SNOW BOUND! 13

CHAPTER THREE   GET TRICKY! 25

CHAPTER FOUR   MEDALS AND MONEY 41

FURTHER READING 45

WEBSITES TO VISIT 45

GLOSSARY 46

INDEX 48

Snowboarding tricks pump up the sport's excitement level.

GET THE GEEK OUT

Snowboarding is not natural. It goes against common sense to challenge gravity with your feet firmly anchored to a speeding plank. Scientists might say that a few of the tricks even twist the laws of **physics**. So, why is it one of the fastest growing winter sports? It's fun—extremely fun!

chapter ONE

Nearly anyone can snowboard. Athletic ability, age and musical taste won't keep you from snowboarding. However, if you're a beginner, it's a good idea to get the geek out before you hit your local snowboard park. This means prepare and practice.

RENT YOUR EQUIPMENT

For starters, plan to rent your snowboard and snowboard boots a day ahead. Borrow snowboard pants, jacket and gloves if you can. Later on, you can sink your savings into the gear.

Call a few rental places to check on prices and packages. You might find deals on lift tickets and lessons, too. At the rental shop, find a trained outfitter to help you. Poorly fitted **equipment** can blow your first day. It can also add pain to the day after. Ask for soft snowboard boots and leave the hard boots for the race team. Soft boots should fit snugly, almost tightly, around your feet. Your heels should not lift up. Expect your outfitter to ask you some basic questions, too:

1. **If you slide across your kitchen floor in stocking feet, which foot leads?**
   Many people lead with their left foot. Snowboarders call that a "regular-footed" stance. You're "goofy-footed" if you lead with the right. Riding goofy isn't bad or wrong, just different.

2. **How tall are you? How much do you weigh?**
   Snowboards should come up somewhere between your shoulders and nose. Weight is more important—yours, and the board's. The outfitter matches the board to your weight range.

3. **How much snowboarding have you done already?**
   Be honest. If you're a star alpine racer, say so. Most renters are new to snowboarding and rental shops usually offer them more forgiving beginner boards and soft boots.

While you're still in the rental shop, try on your boots with the snowboard. Know how your bindings and leash work. Tighten your bindings enough to keep your heels from slipping.

CHA-CHING!

When you decide to invest in equipment, figure on spending between $500 and $950 for a snowboard, bindings, snowboard boots, goggles and gloves. Add another $350 to $550 (or more!) for the jacket, snowboard pants, synthetic underwear and socks. Get a helmet, too—$60 to $135 well spent.

GIRLS: BUY WOMAN'S LAST BOOTS

Girls should buy boots made from a "woman's last," a wooden foot that the boot liner is wrapped around and stitched. Women's calves start lower than men's. Also, women's heels are slimmer, but the balls of their feet are wider. You'll feel an uncomfortable difference if you settle for men's boots.

KNOW YOUR BOARDS

Most shops carry beginning to advanced models of three kinds of snowboards: freestyle, freeride and alpine carve. Used older boards may be twin-tipped (curved the same at each end). Newer boards widen at the nose and taper at the tail.

Freestyle: Light and shapely with stiff tip and tail; used for tricks, jumps and pipe parks.

Freeride: Progressive flex gives a soft tip and stiff tail; preferred for all-purpose and backcountry.

Alpine carve: Stiff! The rounded tip and flat tail carve tight turns and build speed for racing.

Wear snowboard gloves.
They use stronger and warmer fabrics than normal winter gloves. Snowboarders drag their hands in the snow. They grab the metal edge of their boards. They crash. Normal winter gloves can't handle the action.

Remember, a tall, upright stance with straight legs tips over easier than a squat stance with legs apart and knees bent.

RUG RUNNING

Try these carpet-riding tips before you head for the hills:

1. Work The Bindings

Sport shops sell many kinds of bindings, but yours will most likely use a base plate and **ratcheting** straps. They don't release on their own, not even when you fall. Practice working your bindings indoors where it's warm and private.

2. Power Stance

You gain power and control from your stance. It also keeps you upright. Picture a tall, thin vase and a short, squat mug. Which one could you knock over easier? The same physics apply to your stance.

At home, strap both feet in and bend your knees a bit with your weight slightly forward. Face toward your snowboard tip and look straight ahead. Keep your arms and hands ahead near waist level. Put extra **pressure** on your toes or your heels to dig the board's edges down. On snow, you use your toe-edge or your heel-edge pressure to turn.

After you get a feel for the stance, try bending low and rising up in the same form. Your upper body moves very little—the action comes from your knees and legs. This up and down movement helps you balance as you go over bumps.

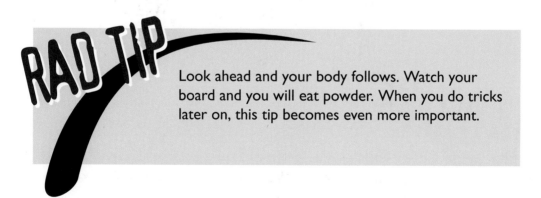

RAD TIP

Look ahead and your body follows. Watch your board and you will eat powder. When you do tricks later on, this tip becomes even more important.

3. Falling Exercises

Why practice falling now when it's sure to happen anyway? Falling correctly prevents injuries. Also, you'll want to know how to get back up without looking (and feeling) silly. The most common snowboard injuries happen to the wrists and lower arms. When you fall forward, tuck and roll! Don't reach out your arms. Instead, try to ball up your fists. This helps cushion the **impact**. When you fall backward, your rear-end plants in the snow. Your head may slap the surface. You'll love your helmet then. If your rear-end fails to plant, and you slide downhill, remember that plowing with your board in front of you will dump a major arc of snow on your head before you stop.

With your feet locked in the bindings, practice your **recovery** move. Always move around to get up toe-side, or facing the hill, so you can see what's coming at you!

4. Walkward Movements

Snowboarders ride a chairlift up the mountain. That's easy. Walking on and off the lift takes more work because it feels so awkward. Practice walking by strapping in only your front foot. Put your weight on the front foot. Push off from the carpet with your back foot, then rest your back foot on the stomp pad between the bindings. You won't glide far on the carpet, but you'll get a feel for the movement. Take little steps. Turning your hips forward helps. Test yourself backwards, too!

RAD TIP

Wear wrist guards and knee and elbow pads on your first day. Most fit under your clothes, so no one will know. Remember, everyone starts snowboarding in the same place: the beginning. Don't let the falls get you down!

Everyone crashes sometime. Try to ball up your fists to cushion the impact.

5. Edge Up On Sideslipping

Edging, or sideslipping, comes in handy for stopping, crossing the slope or moving downhill slowly. On snow, start with your board across the fall line (the imaginary line a ball follows rolling down the slope). At home, strap in both feet and bend your knees. Lean hard on your heels so your toe-edge comes off the carpet. It should feel as if you're starting to sit in a low chair. This heel-edge sideslip, or heel-side turn, works when you're facing downhill. Now lean hard on your toes to bring your heel-edge up. A toe-edge sideslip, or toe-side turn, works when you're facing uphill (you're riding backwards downhill).

RAD TIP

Look ahead and your body follows. Watch your board and you will eat powder. When you do tricks later on, this tip becomes even more important.

SNOW BOUND!

Loud music rips the cold air at the snowboard park. Like a fence, the tunes outline your new playground. But you won't spend much time here at first. The groomed half-pipe, tabletop jumps and other bumps belong to more experienced riders for now.

chapter TWO

After buying a lift ticket, head for a lesson. Your friends may know a lot, but what they know might be wrong. A pro shows you how to use actions (body movement) to create reactions (performance) from the board. With lessons, you cut right to the physics of snowboarding—the how-to and why and why-nots. You improve faster and move onto the half-pipe sooner than if you dawg around by yourself.

LESSON BROWNIE POINTS

Impress your instructor with your vast knowledge of snowboarding history! No one knows for sure who made the very first snowboards. Some boards in Austria date back before World War II.

Most people agree, however, that today's snowboard culture traces its roots to "Snurfers" created by Sherman Poppen in 1965. Surfing was the rage in movies and music then. Already a patent-holding inventor, Poppen bolted two kids' skis together to create a surfing effect on snow. The combination of "snow" and "surf" took off. Check out *Transworld Snowboarding Magazine* for the complete history.

THE TURNING POINTS

No matter how much you read and prepare, you really learn the most with an instructor out on the snow. The carpet-riding makes sense then. Your instructor will cover stance and edging, and explain how you build on those actions to create turns. Turns help you control speed and direction.

Two points to keep in mind:

1. Shoulders ALWAYS face down the hill.
2. Hands stay up where you can see them. If you can't see both hands, you lose strength and control in your form.

RAD TIP

Ask for an instructor certified by the American Association of Snowboard Instructors. AASI instructors use their training to fit their lessons to your skill level and learning style. A private lesson costs more than a group lesson, but it's worth it if you want to learn a lot quickly.

1. Basic Turns

Your body and the board move together. Your body stays fairly upright with knees slightly bent. Your legs work to rotate or twist the snowboard to start the turn.

2. Dynamic Turns

Your body and the board move differently. Your body leans to offset the angle of the board as it rides up on its edge. The higher the edge angle, the further out your body leans.

3. Basic Carved Turns

You and your board move together, but you tilt the board on its edge by pressing your heels or toes into the snow. This makes a sidecut that turns the board, instead of your legs working to turn the board.

4. Dynamic Carved Turns

Your body and the board follow different paths, with the snowboard moving away from you. Your heels or toes press the board edge down to carve the turn. The more your body leans, the greater the edge angle. This offset changes as you shift from side to side through each turn.

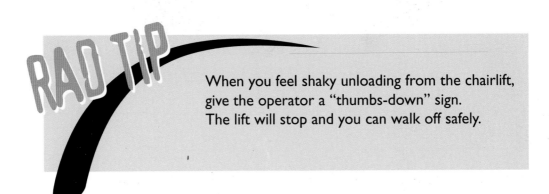

RAD TIP

When you feel shaky unloading from the chairlift, give the operator a "thumbs-down" sign. The lift will stop and you can walk off safely.

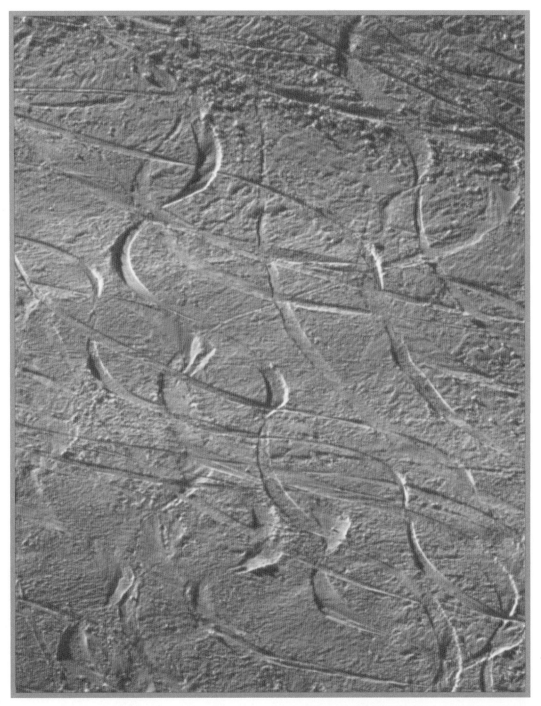

As you improve, you make dynamic carved turns. If you're lucky enough to make "first track" on the slope, you can check how well you carve.

17

The half-pipe competition is one of the most challenging snowboard events.

ON YOUR OWN

Your instructor will set you free to practice your new skills. As you explore the slopes, keep in mind that **courtesy** counts. Share the hills with other snowboarders and with the skiers.

In the past, snowboarders and skiers clashed. Snowboarders earned a **reputation** for rude manners and rule breaking. Resorts banned snowboarding for many years.

THANK 007

Thank James Bond for building the public's interest in snowboarding. The 1985 movie *A View To A Kill* featured wild snowboarding scenes. Audiences loved them. Soon the media swarmed to snowboarding competitions, looking for big air action.

Still, resorts thought snowboarders would chase away their skiing business. Resorts tested the market by building half-pipes for special events, but not for everyday riding. The first man-made half-pipe opened in 1983 for the first World Championship and its shape disappointed riders. It closed after the contest ended.

When the Pipe Dragon slope groomer and other shaping tools became available in the early 1990s, many snowboarders had already moved away from half-pipe riding.

TRIVIA

One Smokin' Half-Pipe
June Mountain at June Lake, California, used hay bales covered with snow to build its half-pipe for the 1989 Op Pro competition. As the riders ran the half-pipe, smoke started to rise out of the snow. The hay had started on fire by itself, melting holes in the snow.

NEW SCHOOL BEGINS

The New School **invasion** began in 1991, probably because riders quit waiting for decent half-pipes. Instead, they rode off picnic tables, downed trees, even junked cars, wherever they found snow.

To bring the snowboarders back, ski resorts began setting aside special places just for snowboarders. Some resorts piped in cool music at their snowboard parks. The snowboarders came.

OLYMPIC ACCEPTANCE

Snowboarding gained its worldwide acceptance when it joined the events at the 1998 Winter Olympics in Nagano, Japan. Today across the U.S., maybe three or four resorts still ban snowboarding. Most welcome snowboarders as long as riders follow the **responsibility** codes posted at the ticket areas.

Now snowboarders—boys and girls, men and women—have shaken off the rebel image. Gray-haired snowboarders play on the slopes with the kids. Smooth Johnson, among the more famous elders, still carved up Squaw Valley on a snowboard at age 70.

YOUR RESPONSIBILITY CODE

1. Always stay in control, and be able to stop or avoid other people and objects.
2. People ahead of you have the right of way. It is your responsibility to avoid them.
3. You must not stop where you obstruct a trail or are not visible from above.
4. Whenever starting downhill or merging into a trail, look uphill and yield to others.
5. Always use devices to help prevent runaway equipment.
6. Observe all posted signs and warnings. Keep off closed trails and out of closed areas.
7. Prior to using any lift, you must have the knowledge and ability to load, ride, and unload safely.

Endorsed by the National Ski Areas Association, Professional Ski Instructors of America, National Ski Patrol, American Association of Snowboard Instructors, American Ski Federations, United States Ski Industries Association, Cross-Country Ski Areas Association, United States Ski Association, Ski Coach's Association and other organizations.

The rebel image shaken, snowboarders are welcome at most ski resorts and the sport has gained worldwide acceptance.

MOVE UP TO BACKCOUNTRY POWDER...SOMEDAY

Ski resorts aren't the only places to snowboard. Snowboarders in the 1970s tried skateboarding tricks while riding down riverbanks or across frozen creek beds. Today's freeriders look for snowy backcountry steeps for nature at its finest—no music, no crowds, no trails. Plenty of boulders, trees and cliffs challenge their every turn.

Many backcountry freeriders use snowshoes or rock-climbing gear to reach the mountaintop. Some drop in from helicopters. When you're really good at snowboarding, you might head to the backcountry too.

DON'T LAUNCH AN AVALANCHE

Even if you're ready for the backcountry, never go alone and do not go out of bounds at the ski resorts. Off-limit areas often include **avalanche** zones. Avalanches kill.

Advanced snowboarders check the avalanche reports. They carry shovels and wear avalanche **transceivers**. These small beepers send out a signal from under the snow to searchers looking for buried victims. Again, avalanches kill. Follow the ski resort rules and take avalanche warnings seriously.

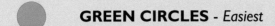 **GREEN CIRCLES** - *Easiest*

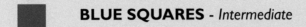 **BLUE SQUARES** - *Intermediate*

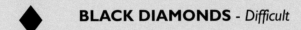 **BLACK DIAMONDS** - *Difficult*

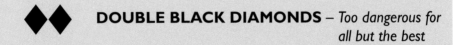 **DOUBLE BLACK DIAMONDS** – *Too dangerous for all but the best*

PRACTICE!
PRACTICE!
PRACTICE!

Go snowboarding.
Go often.
Go further and faster every time.

Most importantly, have fun.

One of the first tricks a snowboarder learns to do in competition is a board grab.

GET TRICKY!

No law says snowboarders must do tricks. But most riders strive for big air, just like on TV.

Start with a few basic tricks and build on them. As you improve, you'll learn that style matters most. Crash, but do it with style. Most often, style means adding your own moves to make your trick more difficult. **Competitors** even lose points if they don't do a grab (not just touching the board, but holding it) while they spin through the air.

chapter

THREE

STRETCH IT OUT

Snowboarders test their muscles every time they ride. Strength and **flexibility** avoid injuries and increase your control. Stretch out, especially before you try tricks. The pros do.

1. **Hamstring and Back Stretch**

   Stand with your legs slightly wider than your shoulders. Raise your arms over your head and inhale. Slowly reach for the ground and exhale as you go. Keep your knees loose. Hold for five seconds. Inhale again on the way up. Repeat three times.

2. **Thighs**

   Lean on your board or a railing. Even better, stand alone to boost your balance. Standing on one foot, bend up the other knee. Wrap your arms around the bent knee and pull your leg up and into your chest. Hold it for five seconds. Lower it and repeat on the other side.

3. **Lunges**

   Stand with your legs apart and knees bent. Slowly bend down on one knee and push back on the other leg. Repeat on the other side.

RAD TIP

Stop snowboarding when you feel tired. Mistakes and injuries happen most often then.

A smart snowboarder knows to stretch prior to hitting the half-pipe.

TRICK TALK

Snowboarding borrows a lot of tricks from skateboarding. For example, the "Fakie to Forward" in snowboarding comes from skateboarding's "half-Cab". The half-Caballerial, named for its inventor, skateboarder Steve Caballero, means to ride backward up the half-pipe or jump, and rotate to land facing forward.

Of course, snowboarders ride with their feet attached to the board. Skateboarders don't. This point feeds an ongoing debate about which sport has harder tricks. Today, most good riders cross between the two sports, taking the edge off the issue.

One more word about tricks: the words may change over time. Names for tricks like the "Chicken Salad" and the "Stalefish" could last forever, but who knows? Although you'll find a glossary with this book, check the Internet sites for the most current (and most hip) words to use.

So what makes a trick sick (awesome)? Remember these three pointers:

1. Smooth action
2. Clean style and plenty of it
3. Stomp the landing

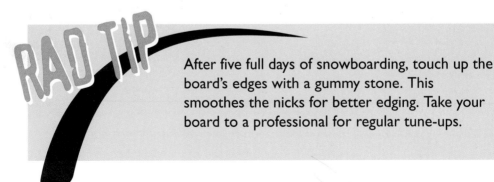

After five full days of snowboarding, touch up the board's edges with a gummy stone. This smoothes the nicks for better edging. Take your board to a professional for regular tune-ups.

Snowboarders use the half-pipe like skateboarders do to get big air. By the end of the season, some half-pipes turn into solid ice. Check the conditions!

BASIC TRICKS

1. Fakie / Switch

Learn to ride backward, or fakie, if you want to do any big air tricks. To do a switch and reverse direction, first turn your head. The shoulders and hips follow. It feels very awkward at first.

2. Frontside and Backside 180

This half-turn to the opposite direction can also save you from eating snow too often. Keep your body upright, with a low edge angle. Rotate the board around its center using power from your legs or entire body. Your legs should stay bent and loose, so they can flex and pump out as you come around. You should end up riding switch.

A good snowboarder has no trouble riding forward or backward, fakie.

A snowboarder performing a tail grab. To add style to a regular tail grab, bend your back leg and bone out your front.

3. Indy Grab

Now you're getting into the true tricks. Carpet-run this one first: move your back hand in-between your feet and grab the toe-edge. It's more of a reach than you think. Move onto the snow and try it off a low jump, or hit, for starters. Then practice tucking so the board comes up to your hand—don't just reach down!

4. Method

Your front arm grabs your heel-edge near your front foot, reaching across the front leg. Again, try this on dry ground first, just to get the feel for it. For added style in the air, bone out (straighten) your back leg. Throw your other hand high in the air.

5. Tail Grab

Your back hand grabs the true tail. Start with both legs bent. Then for more style, do your Tail Grab with your front leg boned out and back leg bent.

INTERMEDIATE TRICKS

1. The Ollie

Invented in the late '70s by skateboarder Allen "Ollie" Gelfand, this trick uses just your feet and momentum to lift you into the air. Stay centered. Pull up on your front leg while shifting your weight to your back leg. Then push off of your back leg and bring your weight back to center.

2. Half-Pipe Fakie to Forward

Don't try this until you can ride fakie easily. Ride fakie off the half-pipe lip and bring your knees up as much as you can while you're in the air. Spread your arms for added style. Turn your head and shoulders where you want your body to follow, so that you land riding forward. Spot your landing in the air and stomp it.

You know you're good when you can land a half-pipe trick riding backward or fakie.

Spin masters are snowboarders who pull off smooth turns in the air.

3. **Backside 360** *(say: Three-Sixty; it means 360 degrees, which is a full circle)*

Riding on your toe-side edge at the jump's lip, turn your head over your back shoulder. Your body follows your head, so stay turned to keep spinning. Spot the landing in the air and come down with your knees slightly bent to cushion the impact.

RAD TIP

Do The Math!

180 (say: One-Eighty) = 180 degrees or a half circle

360 (say: Three-Sixty) = 360 degrees or a full circle

540 (say: Five-Forty) = 540 degrees or a full circle plus a half circle

720 (say: Seven-Twenty) = 720 degrees or two full circles

900 (say: Nine-Hundred) = 900 degrees or two full circles plus a half circle

1080 (say: Ten-Eighty) = 1080 degrees or three full circles - the most spins in a snowboarding trick...so far!

ADVANCED TRICKS

If these tricks sound complicated, that's because they are. They're even more complicated to pull off without crashing. The best tip? Don't try any trick past your skill level. Pushing yourself to improve is good; pushing yourself beyond your limits is dangerous.

You should also know that many ski resorts ban inverted, or upside-down, tricks. So, if your head goes below your board (on purpose) while you're in the air, you risk losing your lift ticket.

Still, you can learn what the advanced tricks look like. Watch for these three moves during competitions:

1. McTwist

Skateboarder Mike McGill created this trick and snowboarders changed it slightly to work in snowy half-pipes. Think of it as a Front Flip 540. Riding up the backside wall, the boarder launches off the lip and turns the shoulders into the pipe to start the flip. Watch for a grab during the rotation. A Mute Grab with the front hand holding the toeside edge between the toes or ahead of the front foot adds style, especially with a leg boned out. After a rotation and a half (540 degrees), the rider stomps the landing riding forward.

Advanced tricks look cool on TV, but they're even more awesome when you see them on the slopes.

2. Backside Rodeo

The rider carves toeside up the kicker on a tabletop jump. Just off the lip the rider's body turns 90 degrees or backwards to the jump. The legs tuck up. For style, the front leg bones out while the front hand holds the backside edge between the bindings in a Melancholy Grab. The rider turns backside another 90 degrees before releasing the grab and landing fakie.

3. Superman Frontflip

Riding toeside on a good-sized jump, the boarder Nollies (like an Ollie, but using the board's nose instead of the tail) off the kicker. The body turns 90 degrees, stretching forward Superman-style. To push into the front flip, the rider whips the front hand overhead and downward. The legs tuck up during the flip until the landing. Most gawkers don't realize the rider actually lands blind.

MEDALS AND MONEY

The 1998 Winter Olympics at Nagano, Japan, gave snowboarding competitions a stamp of approval. Now the Banked Slalom, the U.S. Open, world championships, extreme series, big-air contests, and even judged freeriding attract male and female competitors from all over the world.

chapter

FOUR

These competitions help to create the Pro and Super Pro snowboarders. Sponsors look for winners, but winners with personality. Only a few Super Pros, like Shaun Palmer, Craig Kelly and Terje Haakonsen enjoy full sponsorships and enough money to live well. Other full-time riders, such as pro alpine racers, rarely break even. They pay for their own equipment, training, travel and contest entry fees. They commit themselves to the sport mostly because they love it, no matter the cost.

CHAMPION FOCUS

Craig Kelly

Born: April 1, 1966
Height: 5' 10" (1.8 m)
Weight: 165 lbs. (74.8 kg)

Craig Kelly, one of the sport's first champions, started as a freerider then moved into freestyle and alpine competitions. He learned to snowboard at Mount Baker in Washington in 1981. Craig competed as a pro for the first time in 1985 at the Mount Baker Legendary Banked Slalom. During his career, he won seven World Championships and enough titles to wallpaper a house.

Craig stopped competing in the early 1990s. Now he mainly rides for videos and movies, and concentrates on freeriding all over the world. He also helps develop and test equipment for his sponsors, Burton snowboarding and Oakley optics.

Called a style king of snowboarding, Craig preaches snow safety and avalanche awareness. He also shares his talents in the Burton-sponsored program called Chill, which introduces snowboarding to at-risk kids.

Michele Taggart

Born: May 6, 1970
Height: 5'6" (1.7 m)
Weight: 130 lbs. (60 kg)

Michele Taggart showed potential as snowboarding's leading female champion from the start. A long-time skier, Michele entered her first snowboard contest at Hoodoo Ski Bowl after just three times on a snowboard. She won. The tenth time she went snowboarding, she competed in her first World Cup at Breckenridge, Colorado.

Now a five-time winner of the Overall title, Michele has won more alpine and freestyle contests than any other female snowboarder. She quit racing after breaking her leg. Then she worked back into half-pipe competitions. Except for 1992, she held the U.S. Half-pipe title every year between 1990 and 1995. She kept her focus and became the World Half-pipe Champion in 1998, the same year she joined the U.S. team at the Olympics in Nagano, Japan.

Michele still competes in half-pipe contests during the season. She also spends her time freeriding and riding for photographers.

START LOCAL

Snowboarding competitions pop up all over snow country. The United States **Amateur** Snowboarding Association (USASA) maintains an organized amateur contest schedule. These events at local ski resorts let intermediate and advanced riders test their skills in Half-Pipe, One-Hit Jam, Boardercross and Slopestyle competitions, most often for medals and prizes.

The *USASA* also includes an alpine or racing circuit which moves from resort to resort throughout the winter. Pro racers often rip down the hill faster than 50 miles an hour (80 kph) as they charge around gates, and the amateurs fly by almost as quickly!

RAD TIP

Check your favorite sport shop for local contests. Pros also endorse local shops, the first step to sponsorship.

FURTHER READING

Your library and the Internet can help you learn more about snowboarding. Check these titles and sites for starters:

Armentrout, David. *Sports Challenge: Snowboarding.* Vero Beach, FL: The Rourke Book Company, 1997.

Mammano, Julie. *Rhinos Who Snowboard.* San Francisco: Chronicle Books, 1997.

Miller, Billy, ed. *Ultimate Snowboarding.* Carlton Books, 1998.

Snowboard Manual: Official Instruction Guide of the American Association of Snowboard Instructors. Lakewood, CO: AASI.,1998.

Werner, Doug and Jim Waide. *Snowboarder's Start-Up: A Beginner's Guide to Snowboarding, 2nd Ed.* San Diego: Tracks Publishing, 1998.

WEBSITES TO VISIT

www.boardsnow.com

www.expn.go.com

www.mountainzone.com

www.psia.org

www.physsportsmed.com

www.snowblown.com

www.snowboarding-online.com

GLOSSARY

amateur (AM uh choor) — an athlete who competes for pleasure; they do not receive pay for winning

avalanche (AV uh lanch) — a large area of snow that breaks free and plows down the mountain like a mud slide

competitors (kuhm PET ih turz) — people or teams trying to win a contest

courtesy (KUR tuh see) — polite manners

dynamic (dih NAM ik) — active or energetic movement; in snowboarding, your body and the board follow different paths in a dynamic move

equipment (ih KWIP ment) — gear

flexibility (FLEK sah BILL uh tee) — ability to bend and stretch

impact (IM pakt) — the force of a fall

invasion (in VAY zhun) — an entrance or a take-over

physics (FIZ iks) — the science of matter, energy, motion, and force

pressure (PRESH uhr) — weight or force placed onto an object by pushing or pressing

ratcheting (RACH it ing) — a device using a toothed bar to hold tight or not slip backward

recovery (rih KUV eh ree) — returning to the normal position

reputation (rep yue TA shun) — what people generally think about the character of a person, group or event

responsibility (reh SPON sah BILL ah tee) — a duty; knowing right from wrong

transceivers (tran SEE vurz) — small safety radios that send out beeps to rescue workers

INDEX

alpine   6, 7, 42, 43, 44

American Association of
Snowboard Instructors
(AASI) 15

avalanche   22, 42

Bond, James   19

Caballero, Steve   28

edging   28

equipment   6, 7, 42

falling   9, 10, 12

freeride   7, 22, 41, 42, 43

freestyle   7, 42, 43

Gelfand, Allen "Ollie"   34

half-pipe   13, 19, 20, 28, 34,
43, 44

Kelly, Craig   42

lessons   6, 14

New School   20

outfitter   6

physics   5, 9

Pipe Dragon   19

pressure   9

Responsibility Code   20

sideslipping   12

Snurfers   14

Taggart, Michele   43

transceivers   22

turns   7, 9, 10, 16, 22, 30,
34, 37

United States Amateur
Snowboarding Association
(USASA)   44

woman's last   7

ABOUT THE AUTHOR

Tracy Nelson Maurer specializes in nonfiction and business writing. Her most recently published children's books include the *A to Z* series, also from Rourke Publishing LLC. She lives with her husband Mike and two children in Superior, Wisconsin.